Marta Magellan

Illustrations by Steve Weaver

Pineapple Press, Inc.
Sarasota, Florida

Photo Credits

Note: All photos through istock.com, except those by James Gersing and Marta Magellan. Cover photo of Malayan tiger by James Gersing; Frontispiece photo of male lion by Nico Smit; photos on pages 20 (puma), 38 (puma), 40 (lioness), 44 (puma), and 46 (white Bengal tiger) by James Gersing; photo on page 10 of rare white lion by Marta Magellan; photo of black jaguar on page 8 by Sharon Morris; inserted photo of white domestic cat on page 10 by Aleksandar Nakic; photo on page 12 of male lion by Gez Browning; photos on pages 14 (cheetah) and 26 (cheetah) by Graeme Purdy; photo of leopard on page 16 by Alexander Hafemann; photo of leopard on page 18 by Mark Kostich; photos on pages 22 (Siberian tigress) and 30 (male lion) by Neal McClimon; photo of clouded leopard on page 24 by Dieter Spears; photo of leopard on page 28 by Dirk Freder; photo of tiger on page 32 by Ellen Stenard; photo of tiger on page 34 by Anna Yu; photo of tiger cub on page 36 by Eric Isselée; and photo of snow leopard on page 42 by Yan Gluzberg.

Inquiries should be addressed to:

Pineapple Press, Inc.
P.O. Box 3889
Sarasota, Florida 34230
www.pineapplepress.com

Library of Congress Cataloging-in-Publication Data

Magellan, Marta
Those colossal cats / Marta Magellan ; illustrated by Steve Weaver.
p. cm.
Includes bibliographical references and index.
ISBN 978-1-56164-457-5 (hb : alk. paper) —
ISBN 978-1-56164-458-2 (pb : alk. paper)
1. Felidae—Juvenile literature. I. Weaver, Steve, ill. II. Title.
QL737.C23M243 2009
599.75—dc22
                    2009023032

First Edition
Hb 10 9 8 7 6 5 4 3 2 1
Pb 10 9 8 7 6 5 4 3 2 1

Design by Steve Weaver
Printed in China

To our four children,
who remind us of big cats:
Leon, the lion
Jason, the clouded leopard
Tracy Monique, the tiger cub
Marc Gabriel, the black jaguar

Acknowledgments

Special thanks to: members of my family for helping me with the production of this book; Mauro Magellan for the tiger mask; Tracy Monique Magellan for Photoshop help; and, of course, my husband, James Gersing, for help with many aspects of putting the book together.

I am also grateful to: Tamian Wood for designing the activities; Linda Bernfeld and Elaine Landau along with all the members of the Miami SCWBI critique group for their suggestions; and June Cussen, a truly gracious and wonderful editor.

Contents

What are colossal cats?

Colossal means really huge. All cats, big or small, belong to the same animal family. Because of their size and strength, the big cats fill people with wonder and awe. The biggest cats of all are the **lions**, **tigers**, **leopards**, and **jaguars**. These four are sometimes called "great cats." **Cheetahs**, **snow leopards**, **clouded leopards**, and **pumas** are also big cats. (Pumas are also known as panthers, cougars, or mountain lions.)

What's the difference between big and small cats?

They are alike in many ways. All cats hunt other animals to eat, and all have good eyesight and sensitive whiskers. Their size and strength set big cats apart. They can leap higher and run faster. Small cats hunt mice and lizards. Big cats can hunt and eat large animals, like zebras. That makes them a lot scarier than small cats!

What do big cats eat?

They are carnivores (meat eaters). Big cats can eat any animal, from a mouse to a small elephant. Florida panthers have even been seen eating grasshoppers. But you'll probably never see one eating broccoli! Often big cats hunt animals several times larger than themselves. A big cat can go days without catching and eating anything. They don't eat three meals a day like we do.

DINING ROOM

How do cats hunt?

Cats stalk their prey by hiding in the grass or forest. Cats must chase and catch the animal before it runs away. The cat will hold down the animal with its claws and bite it with its powerful jaws. All big cats except lions hunt alone. The lioness (a female lion) does most of the hunting for the lion family. The male lion sometimes hunts, but he prefers to sit around waiting for someone else to catch his dinner.

Where do big cats live?

Big cats live on most continents except Antarctica, Australia, and Europe. You can find tigers and clouded leopards in the mountains and forests of Asia. Others, like the lion and cheetah, live in the dry grasslands of Africa. Jaguars live in the hot, steamy rainforests and swamps of Central and South America. One big cat, the snow leopard, lives in freezing lands high up in the mountains, even as far north as the Arctic Circle. Where they live is called their habitat.

Do all big cats roar and purr?

Lions, tigers, jaguars, and leopards are the only ones that roar. Pumas, snow leopards, cheetahs, and clouded leopards can't roar, but they can purr without stopping. The roaring cats purr a little, but only between breaths. Cats make sounds to communicate. A roar usually means "stay away." Scientists are still trying to figure out why cats purr. They purr in many situations, not just when they're calm and happy.

Why do cats sleep so much?

Cats are the sleepiest animals in the world. They spend most of the day, 16–20 hours, sleeping or resting. They are saving their energy for hunting. They might wake up for a drink from the river or to play with each other. When the sun sets and it's a little cooler, it's time to hunt. Cheetahs hunt in the daytime, but they sleep between hunts, too. You could say they take catnaps.

Which is the most colossal cat of all?

The largest and strongest of the world's cats is the tiger. To many people, it is also the most beautiful. The Siberian or Amur tiger is the biggest of all. One can weigh over 600 pounds (272 kg) in the wild. One tiger weighs as much as about 13 first graders! There is one cat that is even bigger, the liger, but it's mostly born and lives in zoos. It's a cross between a male tiger and a female lion.

Which is the smallest of the big cats?

The clouded leopard, named for the large cloudlike spots on its fur, is the smallest. It is little compared to a lion or a tiger, but it's still much bigger than a house cat! It is medium-sized and weighs about 33–50 lbs (15–23 kg). If you've never heard of a clouded leopard, it's because they are good at hiding in forests. Only a few people have seen one in the wild.

Which cat is the fastest?

The cheetah is the fastest of all the cats. It is the only cat that can stretch its body completely while its four feet are off the ground. When the cheetah spots its prey, it dashes toward it in great, long strides. It's as if it's *flying*! The cheetah's top speed is around 60 miles per hour (97 km/h), as fast as a car on the highway. It runs that fast only for a few seconds. But that's enough time to catch a speedy gazelle.

Do big cats climb trees?

Yes, they can all climb trees. But lions and tigers aren't very good at it because of their size. Pumas, leopards, and clouded leopards are great climbers. Leopards often drag big prey up a tree to keep other animals away. Clouded leopards can leap from branch to branch. Both leopards and clouded leopards come down from trees headfirst with no trouble. Clouded leopards can even move along a branch by hanging *under* it.

Which cat roars the loudest?

The lion has a fierce roar. It sounds like thunder. The male lion's roar can be heard 5 miles (about 8 kilometers) away. Sometimes whole groups of lions, called prides, will roar together. They are making sure other lions know it's their territory.

Why do tigers have stripes and leopards have spots?

A cat needs camouflage. That means it has to look like the surroundings so its prey can't see it. A tiger's stripes blend with the rays of sunlight coming through the trees and grasses. The leopard's spotted fur makes it hard to see behind a bush. Sometimes jaguars and leopards have spotted black fur. These dark spots help them hide in the dark forest. A snow leopard has light fur that blends into the snowy woods.

Do big cats like to swim?

Most cats don't like water, but pumas, tigers, and jaguars do. Jaguars live and hunt in the swampy grasslands and tropical rainforests of South America. They are often in the water, looking for food. Small reptiles and fish are delicious to jaguars. Tigers seem to enjoy dips in cool water, especially when it's hot. The tigers of Southeast Asia spend much of their time in rivers, feeding on fish and turtles. They are excellent swimmers.

What are big cat babies like?

They are cute! Lion, tiger, jaguar, and leopard babies are called cubs. All other cat babies are called kittens. They are born blind. Their eyes open in ten to fourteen days. Some cubs and kittens have different markings from their parents. Lion cubs and puma kittens have spots that later disappear. Cubs and kittens are very playful. They pounce on each other and anything that moves. That teaches them hunting skills.

How do cats see so well?

Cats have 3-D vision, like people. Not all animals do. Cats can see well at night, too. In very dim light they can see a lot better than people can. Their pupils, the dots in the middle of their eyes, open up when it's dark. The pupils close to a slit or small dot when it's bright. Have you seen cat eyes glowing in the dark? That's because cats have a mirror-like layer behind their eyes that shines when light is aimed at them.

Why do cats lick their fur?

Cats like to be clean. Since they don't use soap and water like people, cats lick their fur to wash themselves. Their tongues feel like sandpaper. Members of the same family often clean each other. They are showing that they belong together. They are also putting their smell on the family member. Licking also helps to keep cats cool when it's hot outside.

Which big cat is the furriest?

Male lions have the furriest heads. The fur around their heads is called a mane. Snow leopards are the furriest all over. They live in some of the coldest places on Earth, so their fur needs to be thick and long to protect them. A snow leopard curls its thick, wooly tail around itself when lying down during really cold weather. It's like a long, warm scarf.

Can a big cat be a pet?

There are people who keep even the largest cats as pets. Usually they do it because cubs and kittens are so cute and adults so awesome. Even when raised by humans from birth, big cats are still wild animals, and they grow up to be colossal wild animals. They can hurt you just by playing with you. Big cats also need a lot of space to roam. It's better to see them at the zoo.

Are big cats endangered?

Here's a sad fact: all the big cats are rare or endangered. Most of the wild cats are losing their habitats as people move into the places cats once roamed. The tiger will probably be the first of the big cats to become extinct (no more) in the wild. Wild tigers are so rare they are almost gone. Today more tigers live in zoos than in their natural habitats. Zoos and animal reservations are helping to keep these magnificent animals from total extinction.

Activities
Make a tiger mask

Tiger Mask

- Ask a grown-up to photocopy the tiger mask onto card stock (stiff paper).
- Make the photocopy 20 percent bigger (so that it'll fit over your face).
- Color the mask any way you like.
- Cut carefully around the mask and cut out the eye holes (or ask a grown-up).
- Punch small holes through the red dots on either side of the mask.
- Thread 12 inches of shoestring, ribbon, or a piece of elastic through each hole.
- Tie a knot on the front side of the mask so the ribbon won't slip through.
- To wear the mask, tie the ribbons or shoestrings together at the back of your head.

Make big cat finger puppets

Color your own finger puppets

Lions and Tigers and Leopards! Oh my! Have fun coloring your own finger puppets. Don't forget their bodies and tails. One is left blank so you can draw in your own cat face.

Make a copy on a copy machine.
Color the puppets.
Have an adult cut out the puppet shape.
Cut carefully along the red dotted line around the head.
Bend the puppet around your finger and tape flap "a" to flap "b."

Where to learn more about big cats

Books

Brakefield, Tom. *Kingdom of Might: The World's Big Cats.* Stillwater, Minnesota: Voyageur Press, 1993.

Guggisberg, C. A. W. *Wild Cats of the World.* New York: Taplinger Publishing Company, 1975.

Landau, Elaine. *Big Cats: Hunters of the Night.* Animals after Dark series. New York: Enslow Elementary, 2007.

Simon, Seymour. *Big Cats.* New York: HarperTrophy, 1994.

Walker, Sarah. *Big Cats.* New York: DK Publishing, 2002.

Websites
www.thebigcats.com
www.bigcats.com
www.lairweb.org.nz/tiger
www.bigcatrescue.org
www.lionresearch.org/main.html
(Lion Research Center)

Glossary

camouflage – fur colors that blend in with the surroundings in order to hide the animal

captivity – living inside a limited area like a cage or a house; not in the wild

carnivore – type of animal that eats meat

colossal – really, really big

endangered – animals in danger of becoming extinct; not many left in the wild

extinct – no longer existing

feline – relating to the cat family of carnivorous predators

female – girl

gazelle – a very speedy, deer-like animal from Africa

habitat – the place where an animal lives and grows

male – boy

mane – the long hair around an animal's head, like that on a male lion

predators – animals that kill other animals for food

prey – the animals that are killed and eaten by other animals.

pride – a family of lions that lives and hunts together

pupil – the black area of the eye that opens and closes

rare – very few existing in the world

species – a particular kind of plant or animal

stalk – to hunt for prey secretly

surroundings – things that are around, such as trees in a forest or sand in a desert

survive – to stay alive

About the author

Marta Magellan is a nature lover who teaches English, Creative Writing, and Survey of Children's Literature at Miami Dade College. An avid admirer of wildlife, she travels often to Brazil and wherever else she can find a wilderness. She lives in Miami, Florida, with her husband, James Gersing, who took some of the photographs in this book.

Index

(Numbers in **bold** refer to photographs.)

Here are the other books in this series. For a complete catalog, visit our website at www.pineapplepress.com. Or write to Pineapple Press, P.O. Box 3889, Sarasota, Florida 34230-3889, or call (800) 746-3275.

Those Amazing Alligators by Kathy Feeney. Illustrated by Steve Weaver, photographs by David M. Dennis. Discover the differences between alligators and crocodiles; learn what alligators eat, how they communicate, and much more. Ages 5–9.

Those Beautiful Butterflies by Sarah Cussen. Illustrated by Steve Weaver. This book answers 20 questions about butterflies—their behavior, why they look the way they do, how they communicate, and much more. Ages 5–9.

Those Delightful Dolphins by Jan Lee Wicker. Illustrations by Steve Weaver. Learn the difference between a dolphin and a porpoise, find out how dolphins breathe and what they eat, and learn how smart they are and what they can do. Ages 5–9.

Those Excellent Eagles by Jan Lee Wicker. Illustrated by Steve Weaver, photographs by H. G. Moore III. Learn all about those excellent eagles—what they eat, how fast they fly, why the American bald eagle is our nation's national bird. Ages 5–9.

Those Funny Flamingos by Jan Lee Wicker. Illustrated by Steve Weaver. Learn why those funny birds are pink, stand on one leg, eat upside down, and much more. Ages 5–9.

Those Lively Lizards by Marta Magellan. Illustrated by Steve Weaver, photographs by James Gersing. In this book you'll meet lizards that can run on water, some with funny-looking eyes, some that change color, and some that look like little dinosaurs. Ages 5–9.

Those Magical Manatees by Jan Lee Wicker. Illustrated by Steve Weaver. Twenty questions and answers about manatees—you'll find out more about their behavior, why they're endangered, and what you can do to help. Ages 5–9.

Those Outrageous Owls by Laura Wyatt. Illustrated by Steve Weaver, photographs by H. G. Moore III. Learn what owls eat, how they hunt, and why they look the way they do. You'll find out what an owlet looks like, why horned owls have horns, and much more. Ages 5–9.

Those Peculiar Pelicans by Sarah Cussen. Illustrated by Steve Weaver, photographs by Roger Hammond. Find out how much food those peculiar pelicans can fit in their beaks, how they stay cool, and whether they really steal fish from fishermen. Ages 5–9.

Those Terrific Turtles by Sarah Cussen. Illustrated by Steve Weaver, photographs by David M. Dennis. You'll learn the difference between a turtle and a tortoise, and find out why they have shells. Meet baby turtles and some very, very old ones, and even explore a pond. Ages 5–9.

Those Voracious Vultures by Marta Magellan. Illustrated by Steve Weaver, photographs by James Gersing and Ron Magill. Learn all about vultures—the gross things they do, what they eat, whether a turkey vulture gobbles, and more. Ages 5–9.